Raquel and the Letter **R**

Alphabet Friends

by Cynthia Klingel and Robert B. Noyed

The Child's World®

The Child's World®

Published in the United States of America
by The Child's World®
P.O. Box 326
Chanhassen, MN 55317-0326
800-599-READ
www.childsworld.com

The Child's World®: Mary Berendes, Publishing Director

Editorial Directions, Inc.: E. Russell Primm, Editorial
Director; Emily Dolbear, Line Editor; Ruth Martin,
Editorial Assistant; Linda S. Koutris, Photo Researcher
and Selector

Photographs ©: Stockbyte/Punchstock: Cover & 9, 18;
Bob Rowan; Progressive Image/Corbis: 10; Photodisc/
Getty Images: 13; Corbis: 14, 21; Eyewire/Photodisc/
Punchstock: 17.

Library of Congress Cataloging-in-Publication Data
Klingel, Cynthia Fitterer.
  Raquel and the letter R / by Cynthia Klingel and
Robert B. Noyed.
    p. cm. — (Alphabet readers)
Summary: A simple story about a girl named Raquel
who loves living by a river introduces the letter "r".
  ISBN 1-59296-108-8 (Library Bound : alk. paper)
  [1. Rivers—Fiction. 2. Alphabet.] I. Noyed, Robert B., ill.
II. Title.
  PZ7.K6798Raq 2003
  [E]—dc21   2003006609

Note to parents and educators:

The first skill children acquire before becoming successful readers is individual letter recognition. The Alphabet Friends series has been created with the needs of young learners in mind. Each engaging book begins by showing the difference between the capital letter and the lowercase letter. In each of the books on the vowels and the consonants c and g, children are introduced to the different sounds that the letter can make. Finally, children see that the letters can be found at the beginning of a word, in the middle of a word, and in most cases, at the end of a word.

Following the introduction, children meet their Alphabet Friends. The friend in each story encounters many words that include the featured letter of that book. Each noun that begins with the title letter is highlighted in red with the initial letter of the word in bold. Above the word is a rebus drawing that establishes a strong picture cue.

At the end of each book, we have included three words lists. Can your young learners find all the words in each book with the title letter in them?

Let's learn about the letter **R.**

The letter **R** can look like this: **R.**

The letter **R** can also look like this: **r.**

The letter **r** can be at the beginning of a word, like raincoat.

raincoat

The letter **r** can be in the middle of a word, like kangaroo.

kanga**r**oo

The letter **r** can be at the

end of a word, like hair.

hai**r**

Raquel lives by the **r**iver. She can see

the **r**iver from her **r**oom. **R**aquel has many

things to do by the **r**iver.

Raquel listens to the **r**iver. When the

water runs rapidly, it seems as if the

river is roaring.

Raquel likes to throw **r**ocks in the **r**iver.

The **r**ocks make **r**ipples in the **r**iver. **R**aquel

likes to run her toes through the **r**ipples.

Raquel watches animals that live by the

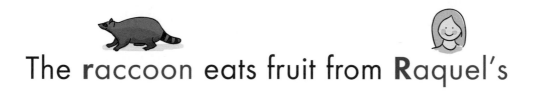

river. A **r**accoon lives near the **r**iver.

The **r**accoon eats fruit from **R**aquel's

garden. **R**aspberries are his favorite.

Raquel likes to float on the **r**iver in a **r**aft.

The **r**aft is big enough for **R**aquel and a

friend! They relax in the **r**aft on the **r**iver.

17

Raquel loves rainy days by the **r**iver.

She wears her **r**aincoat and her rubber

boots. She still loves to run in the **r**iver.

Raquel sees a **r**ainbow over the **r**iver.

The **r**ainbow comes after the rainy day.

Raquel loves her life on the **r**iver.

Fun Facts

A **r**accoon is a furry animal with a bushy tail. The black hair around its eyes looks like a mask. A **r**accoon's front paws are very sensitive to touch and can pick up objects skillfully. Sometimes **r**accoons look as if they're washing their food because they will dunk it in water or explore their food with their paws. The name **r**accoon comes from the Native American word *arakun,* meaning "he who scratches with his hands."

Have you ever tried to find a **r**ainbow? A **r**ainbow is an arc of colors that appears when the sun shines through raindrops. Therefore, **r**ainbows can only appear in a part of the sky where there is still rain. If you do find a **r**ainbow, show a friend. But if your friend stands next to you, he or she won't see the same **r**ainbow. From a different point of view, your friend will see a different set of raindrops in the sky, and therefore a different **r**ainbow!

To Read More

About the Letter R
Klingel, Cynthia. *Rusty Red: The Sound of R.* Chanhassen, Minn.: The Child's
   World, 2000.

About Raccoons
Nelson, Kristin L. *Clever Raccoons.* Minneapolis: Lerner Publications, 2000.
Ring, Elizabeth, and Dwight Kuhn (photographer). *The Little Raccoon.* New York:
   Random House, 2001.
Willis, Nancy Carol. *Raccoon Moon.* Middleton, Del.: Birdsong Books, 2002.

About Rainbows
Fowler, Allan. *All the Colors of the Rainbow.* Danbury, Conn.: Children's Press,
   1998.
Schwartz, Betty Ann. *What Makes a Rainbow?* Santa Monica, Calif.: Piggy Toes
   Press, 2000.

Words with R

Words with R at the Beginning

raccoon
raft
rainbow
raincoat
rainy
rapidly
Raquel
raspberries
relax
ripples
river
roaring
rocks
room
rubber
run
runs

Words with R in the Middle

are
favorite
friend
from
fruit
garden
kangaroo
learn
raspberries
roaring
through
throw
wears
word

Words with R at the End

after
for
hair
her
letter
near
over
river
rubber
water

About the Authors

Cynthia Klingel has worked as a high school English teacher and an elementary teacher. She is currently the curriculum director for a Minnesota school district. Cynthia Klingel lives with her family in Mankato, Minnesota.

Robert B. Noyed started his career as a newspaper reporter. Since then, he has worked in communications and public relations for a Minnesota school district for more than fourteen years. Robert B. Noyed lives with his family in Brooklyn Center, Minnesota.